KiLLER

Published by Barrington Stoke
An imprint of HarperCollins*Publishers*
1 Robroyston Gate, Glasgow, G33 1JN

www.barringtonstoke.co.uk

HarperCollins*Publishers*
Macken House, 39/40 Mayor Street Upper,
Dublin 1, DO1 C9W8, Ireland

First published in 2025

ISBN 978-0-00-876490-6

10 9 8 7 6 5 4 3 2 1

A catalogue record for this book is available from the British Library

Printed and bound in India by Replika Press Pvt. Ltd.

KILLER

TANYA LANDMAN

ILLUSTRATED BY
Alessandro Valdrighi

Barrington Stoke

For good dogs everywhere

NOW

Stones mark an old grave. An important one.

Who’s buried there? A prince? A king?

Read on. The answer may surprise you.

THEN

It was a bad winter that year. Cold. Grey. Wet.

Snow, then rain. So much rain.

Water fell from the skies day after day. Night after night.

And then spring came. A dry, sunny day. The air clear and fresh.

The prince wanted to go on a hunt.

"It's a good day to be alive!" he shouted.

"A good day to ride!"

"A good day to hunt!"

"Saddle the horses!"

"Call the hounds!"

He turned to his lady. “Today we ride! You and I. Together.”

“Who will look after our baby?” she asked.

"Gelert, our brave dog!" he said. "No man or maid could take better care of him than Gelert!"

The hunting party set out. It was a fast ride. A good hunt. They would feast well that night.

But coming home – blood. Blood! Blood! Walls splashed with it. Floors wet with it.

And the dog Gelert. Fur soaked with blood. Teeth dripping with blood. Whose blood?

“Where is our baby?” called the prince.

Nowhere to be found!

“Gelert has eaten our baby!” he yelled.

Red hot anger. Ice cold hate. The prince swung his sword. A sudden blow.

A puzzled look. A sad whimper. Gelert wags his tail one last time.

Silence. For one, two, three beats of the heart.

But then … a soft cry. A baby's cry? From under the cradle! The baby safe. Not hurt.

Again the question: whose blood? Whose?

There! A wolf! A wild wolf had crept into the castle. A wolf that came to kill and eat the baby.

A wolf, killed by Gelert. The baby saved by him. Such a good dog. A loyal dog. A lovely dog.

But now a dead dog. Killed by his master.

Grief. Pain. Sorrow. A sadness that would never fade.

They buried Gelert as a hero.

They buried Gelert as if he was a prince or a king.

His grave is still marked with stones.

His master is all but forgotten.

But the story of Gelert will live for ever.

Our books are tested for children and young people by children and young people.

Thanks to everyone who consulted on a manuscript for their time and effort in helping us to make our books better for our readers.